POEMS
OF
LOVE
AND
WHIMSY

HAROLD NIGHTINGALE

Poems of Love and Whimsy
Copyright © 2022 by Harold Nightingale

All rights reserved. No part of this publication may be reproduced, distributed, or transmitted in any form or by any means, including photocopying, recording, or other electronic or mechanical methods, without the prior written permission of the author, except in the case of brief quotations embodied in critical reviews and certain other non-commercial uses permitted by copyright law.

Tellwell Talent
www.tellwell.ca

ISBN
978-0-2288-5446-3 (Paperback)

Contents

Preface to Poems of Love and Whimsy v
Reflections on a Winter Afternoon vii
Dance With Me 1
You Never Said My Songs Were Good 3
That Old Dusty Road 4
I've Never Known a Wonder 5
Little Love Rhymes 7
Memorial for Ellen 8
A Rose Of Any Hue 9
The Boy Within 10
Four Fun Rhymes 11
A Valentine Limerick to Josi 11
Anniversary 2005 11
Ode to a Voyageur's Lady 12
Thoughts of a Fortunate Man 12
Fear and Pride...the Destroyers 13
If you asked me what life is all about, I would say 14
I Believe in Some Fundamental Truths As A Guide For Living 15
The Silence and the Storm 16
On Returning from Madrid 17
My World Is Not The Same 19
Bloor Street (Toronto) 20
On Thought 21
Thought Stream 22
To Monique 24
Blue Rapids 25

Mountain	26
Is It My Imagination?	27
Upsetting My Tranquility	28
Rap for a Valentine	30
Night Errands	32
Times Ephemeral	34
Yesterday~Today~Tomorrow	35
Rose Buds	36
My Kiss Is In The Wind	37

Preface to Poems of Love and Whimsy

In early 2010 I was going through my old papers and boxes when I discovered three brown envelopes in which there were some 150 poems that I had written over the past sixty years...going right back to my high school days. These were in addition to several others I had written more recently...most of the latter being inspired by my wonderful love affair with my wife, Josi.

From this long list of options, Josi and I selected some thirty-five or so to put into print and share with family and friends.

I recognized that, to a large extent, the poems documented significant events or insights I experienced over the years. They certainly identified what was important to me at the time each of them was written. In a very real way they took me on a journey down memory lane that I otherwise could never have enjoyed...and allowed me to experience again the emotions that the events raised in me.

In a pure sense some of what I have written here is not poetry. They might be regarded as "thought streams" or "lyric prose". My purpose in including them is that I have some faint hope that my grandchildren or great grandchildren will read them and thereby experience some insights. (It's too late for my children.) Finally, I decided that publishing these poems would be a wonderful way to celebrate my life...taking my cue from Walt Whitman ("Leaves of Grass") to "celebrate myself". Mine has been a wonderfully full, active, and exciting life that is now drawing to a close. Even so, I continue to meet and enjoy wonderful people as I graduate to experiencing the "palliative care" category.

I owe much thanks to all who inspired me over the years, and to those who more recently encouraged me in this endeavour...especially to Josi who has been a marvellous helpmate in making all this happen.

Harold Nightingale

P.S. Seven of these poems have been put to music and are sung by Mike Cox on a CD yet to be released upon an unsuspecting public.... an excellent example of having great fun with great people while carefully avoiding getting rich.

Reflections on a Winter Afternoon

My beloved Josi;

I sit here looking, from my vantage point in the dining room, out across the frozen river. I see the sun reflecting brilliantly off the snow on the river and off the white base of the light house.

The sparsely wooded mountains, beyond the gleaming shoreline of the opposite bank, seem to huddle protectively around the darkly wooded valley squeezed between their base and the wide river.

Our white birch gleams in the sunlight. A deep fluffy rail of snow defines the balcony while glistening white diamonds swirl down and away from the roof and snow laden branches.

My God of Nature has surrounded me with beauty.

I look across these rooms and see delicate bouquets of dried flowers, ethereal in their array of muted tones. Each has its own silhouette of memories...these are from your summer garden; these are your anniversary roses; these are your wedding bouquet, and those are your collection from an autumn hike.

Everywhere is evidence of loving care, of practicality presented in artful form.

Photographs of our lives are arranged subtly beside creative expressions of ourselves, our lives, and our living.

Your painting tantalizes me...seductive in its form and tone; exciting in its colours.

My Goddess of Love, too, has surrounded me with beauty.

Oh, how much I love this place!...but, oh, how much more I love you!

Harold

Dance With Me

To: Josi

Come!
Dance with me.
Move to the pulse
of our hearts;
Leap with the strength
of our love;
Turn with the spin
of our thoughts;
Sway with the tides
of our lives.

Bending, rising, swooping, swaying...
Inspired by our joy...
We dance...
Eternally, magically, joyfully...

Forever immune against the buffets and the strains,
and the losses and the pains.

You are my partner
in the Dance of Love;
The only dance
worth doing.

Come!...dance with me.

Date: 2 June 2006
Footnote: Written on the night of Friday, 2 June 2006, in the Best Western Inn & Suites in Woodstock, New Brunswick....the night before the final 1200 km leg back to Ottawa on my motorcycle trip alone to visit a dying friend in Nova Scotia. This typed version reflects a couple of changes I made on Saturday, 17 June, 2006.

Josi – Nov 1990 – Sparks Street

You Never Said My Songs Were Good

You never said my songs were good
Or that you liked the rhyme;
Instead, you softly asked me
If I'd sing them one more time.

You never said the words rang true
Or that you liked the tune;
Instead, you softly asked me
If I'd sing them for you soon.

And as you listened to my song,
My song was in your eyes;
And on your lips were gentle words
That made me realize

That sometime we had shared those words
Before the words were there;
And long before the song was born,
The love we shared was there.

Date: 26 Feb 1974
Footnote: I wrote this on Air Canada Flight 160 from Calgary to Toronto. I dedicated it to my dear friends Bert and Lorna Richards following my 40th birthday party at their home on 8 Feb 1974.

That Old Dusty Road

Oh, I've been on this lone
Dusty road for too long,
And I want to have someone to share;
Yes, I've been on this old
Lonely road for too long,
And I need to have someone to care.

So please take my hand;
Turn your face to the wind
And we'll walk down
This road to the end.

I will give you the sunrise
From high silent peaks,
And the soft spray of oceans
To play at your feet.

I will give you the sea,
And the sun and the sand;
And the love of my heart,
And the strength of my hand.

So, please take this ring
And your place in my heart;
Then rest there for ever
In that place in my heart.

Date: 13 April 1992
Footnote: I wrote this before proposing to Josi at the top of Mount Tremblant while spring skiing.

I've Never Known a Wonder

I've seen the mountains rising
In the golden western skies;
I've seen the black loon dancing
And heard its mournful cries.
But I've never seen a wonder
Like the love glow in your eyes.
No, I've never seen a wonder
Like the love glow in your eyes.

I've seen the northern forest,
Heard the lone wolf's baleful cry;
And the Northern Lights have thrilled me
With their splendor in the sky.
But I never saw a wonder
Like the love glow in your eye.
No, I never saw a wonder
Like the love glow in your eye.

I've seen the prairies stretching
For as far as I could see;
And I've often faced the biting wind
As the tempest tossed the sea.
But I never felt a wonder
Like the love you gave to me.
No, I never felt a wonder
Like the love you gave to me.

Well, I've had a million feelings
As I gave this life a try;
Though I loved and lost a hundred times,
'twas seldom that I'd cry.
For I'd never known a wonder
Like the love you gave to me.
No, I'd never known a wonder
Like the love you gave to me.

Date: 20 May 1973
Music-1974

Little Love Rhymes

Josi;
I'm glad we met, I'm glad we wed;
I'm glad for all the joys we've had.
I'm glad I'm yours, I'm glad your mine;
I'm glad you fell for my opening line.

Date: Wedding Anniversary, 9 Oct 1998

Josi;
Everything I see
I want to see with you;
Everything I feel
I want to feel with you;
Every thought I think
I want to share with you;
Everything I love
I want enriched by you;
Every day I live
I want to live with you.

All my love.
Date: Wedding Anniversary 9 Oct 1999

Memorial for Ellen

To Josi...on Ellen

Weep not, my love, for Ellen;
She has flown the grasp
Of care and pain and fear.

Weep not, my love, for things
You dreamed...that might have been
They lie beyond our sphere.

But weep, weep well, my love
For words denied to parting friends,
Farewells a sojourner would hear.

Date: 22 March 1999
On Ellen's death

A Rose Of Any Hue

To: Josi

A rose may come
In any hue,
But none as beautiful
As you.
And, no matter what
Its hue,
I'd rather snuggle up
With you.

Date: 13 Aug 2007
Footnote: On her birthday, I gave my wife Josi a dozen roses and this poem.

The Boy Within

What let me chase
My boyhood dreams
To sail the seas
and bike my country's roads;
To ski her mountain tops
and stalk the northern ox;
To dare the raging river
and the rapid's rocks?
It was the boy within.

Why did I know
My body was
the temple of my mind;
If I was true
I'd have the strength of nine;
Not to make decisions
based upon a fear;
And nothing tried is nothing done?
Because I had the boy within.

How did I bear
The roughest shocks
when illness racked my core;
The foul deceits of evil men
and win out in the end;
and with a grin and with a jest
survive and know I'd done my best?
Because I kept the boy within.

Date: 6 March 2010

Four Fun Rhymes

A Valentine Limerick to Josi

Each Valentine Day's a big plus,
So I do like to make a big fuss.
'cause before the day's out
we'll be tossing about
With only your perfume between us.

Date: 14 Feb 2007

Anniversary 2005

To Josi
You fill my mind
With wonder;
You fill my soul
With love;
But tell you now
I must,
You fill my bod
With lust.

Date: 9 Oct 2005

Ode to a Voyageur's Lady

I'll leave my paddle
Outside your door,
And creep across
Your boudoir's floor.
With pleading voice
I shall implore
"Please kiss me now
...and ever more".

Ik hou van je

Date: 13 Aug 2004, Josi's birthday

Thoughts of a Fortunate Man

To: Josi
Because you are you.
Because you make the good days
even better;
Because you make the bad days into
good ones;
Because you make today better than
yesterday;
Because you make me look forward
to tomorrow;
Because I love you with
every atom in my body,
every thought in my mind.
And just because...
I love you.

Date: 30 Oct 2007

Fear and Pride...the Destroyers

Fear prevents us from doing what we really want a do. So, in another way does pride.

Together, they are devastating....and together have ruined more lives than all man's wars.

Fear prevents us from doing what we need to do to realize our dreams...from being bold enough to make it happen.

Pride prevents us from being close to others...cutting us off from human intercourse.

They work slowly, but they work surely....and they destroy completely.

Date: 1975

If you asked me what life is all about, I would say

Life is about whatever you want it to be about. It is your choice. Not everyone will make the same choice, and nor should they. Just be sure that you, and not someone else, makes the choice for you. And remember, you must also choose the value system that goes with this choice..and this is the most difficult part of the choice to change later in life.

Date: 24 March 2010

I Believe in Some Fundamental Truths As A Guide For Living

I Believe that not living life fully is a far greater loss than death itself.

I Believe that everything is negotiable except my honor and my good name.

I Believe that "love" should be regarded as a verb...that if you love someone you demonstrate it by taking some action, by doing something.

I Believe that the key to survival and to true peace and contentment is to surround yourself with love...daring to accept love and to give love freely and unconditionally.

Date: 2002

The Silence and the Storm

This is my land
and
I am in this land
and
This land is in me.

Should I turn blind,
My eyes
Shall revel still
In memories of
Her vibrant hues,

Should I fall lame,
My mind
Shall follow still
Her shaded trails
And wandering streams

Should I find death,
My spirit
Shall find refuge
In her silence and her storms

For I am in this land
And this land is in me.

Date: 24 Dec 1977

On Returning from Madrid

I remember
Tree spotted hills rolling
into far off mountains:
And narrow cobbled lanes
my arms can span;
...and eyes so dark
I can not see their depth.

I feel
The breath of a walled city
older than my faith;
And winds of a past
that has not died;
...and a mind that
I can almost touch.

I sense
Old genes wrestling with
the mutations of time;
And echoes not yet ready
to desert their ancient ruins;
...and a spirit opening
to fullness in the sun

I hear
Flamenco songs danced
to clapping hands;
And wailed to sad drifting chords
from orange guitars;
...and a voice that tells me
things I did not know before;

I taste
Old recipes and new beginnings
in musty basement caves;
And wine from a soil
aged in endless hope;
..and the loneliness
of dreams denied.

I remember
Spain and wine
and music and sunshine;
...and Janet.

Date: 8 April 1975
Footnote: I wrote this on the plane back from Madrid and Seville.

My World Is Not The Same

You touched my hand
And spoke my name.
And now my world
Is not the same.

Now, your body fills
The memory of my arms.
And in my sleep, it seems
Your scented hair flows
Softly cross my dreams.

Now, your eyes soft light
The hallways of my mind;
And when I think your name,
It echoes lonely through
The canyons of my brain

My world
Is not the same.

My world,
My world,
Is not the same.

Date: 30 October 1972-words
26 April 1973-music

Bloor Street (Toronto)

The sleek black limousine
Moves slowly down the crowded street.
A man, cloaked in stainless steel
And darkly tinted glass, is immune
To the smells and sounds and dust
Of the street.

A boy on a bicycle
Darts quickly through the traffic,
Clad in a wind jacket,
His flying coat tails revealing
Faded jeans with ragged seams,
And shoes down at the heels.

The boy on the bicycle
Peers quickly through the tinted glass
And past the stainless steel
To another world he does not know,
And wonders how he might get in.

The man in the limousine
And the thousand dollar suit
Sees the flying coat tails,
And, choking on the smells and dust of memory,
Wonders how he got in.

Date: 1971
Footnote: When I was a teen I delivered for a store on Bloor St. Twenty years later I was the man in the limousine.

On Thought

Man was blessed with the power to reason for himself.
Nothing new or great comes from him who echoes another's thoughts.
We must think and, ultimately, we must think alone.

Oh would that man some time would take
To stop alone and contemplate
In some place quiet and serene.
A dingy room or mountain scene,
It matters not.

To lift his mind above the stink
And smog and lust of life...and think!
On Man, on Love, Philosophy,
On God, or one's own destiny,
It matters not.

That, as the mole who reaches day,
He might not be, on Judgement Day,
So blinded by the light of Truth,
He's forced to say, like thoughtless youth,
"I never thought...."

So echo not what others say;
For then ye be no more than they,
The barren hills...but nay,
For they at least have strength to stay.

Date: July 1956
Footnote: I was working out of Levis Dockyard doing acceptance tests on the new St. Laurent class Destroyer.

Thought Stream

Life does not come to me
In neat little packages
Not any more.
Things are not
Nicely bundled
With labels

Printed:
"Good" and "Bad"
"Unjust" and "Just"
"Love" and "One" and "Always"
"Happiness" and "Forever"

Life pours like a stream
In Spring flood,
Carrying everything in a jumble
Along with it.

I do not swim
Against the current.
I let it wash over me,
And I do not try
To sort the goodness
From the badness.
And when I think about it
I do not want to.

It is all reality.

I have become
The child
Of consciousness
And the nomad
Of experiences.

For I can not
Put down anchor
In a quiet bay.
I must let life's torrent
Carry me
To the sea of
Infinite awareness
And ultimate reality.

Then maybe,
Just maybe
When you ask me
About Life
I will be able to tell you…

For I will have been there.

Date: 20 May 1973
Footnote: I wrote this on Air Canada flight # 871 from Paris to Montreal (747).

To Monique

A pretty girl in a red dress
Smiled and spoke with me awhile:
She brightened up my dreary day,
Then said good bye and went her way.

I like pretty girls who smile easily;
And perhaps we made each other glad.
It would have been a cheerless trip,
But with her smile, she made joy of it.

Date: 20 May 1973
Footnote: I was returning from Munich through Paris to Montreal on Air Canada flight # 871 on 20 May 1973. An Air Canada hostess saw me working on "Thought Stream" and asked if I would write something for her. So I did. The red dress is her Air Canada uniform.

Blue Rapids

Look at them swirl, brother.
Look.
They rip and toss and bound
Off the rocks;
Sucking on the canyon wall,
Roaring the river's
Challenge call.

No turning back, brother.
Look.
We're in the chute,
Buried in the roar and madness,
Tossing on the crest.
Now comes the boil...
We'll need your best.

Bend your paddle, brother.
Strain
And rage against the sound;
Lift our bark above
The torrent and the foam,
Lest they rise and claim us
For their own.

Well done, my brother.
Look.
We've dodged the swirling vortex
And the danger's all behind.
Now we drift in quiet pools
And raise our paddles o'r our heads
And cheer like crazy fools.

Date: 1975
Footnote: This commemorates an adventure with Noel on the south branch of the French River.

Mountain

Yesterday she was not mine;
She scorned and mocked me,
Threw me down.
And chilled me with her ice.
Her cold breath railed against me;
She howled rejection of me.
Yesterday she was not mine.

Today she is mine.
Now she speaks with warmth
And softer voice, parades her beauty,
And wears the sun like jewels.
Responding sensually to my skis,
She tells me I'm her master now
Today she is mine.

And for one gorgeous day
My mountain and me
We had a love affair
That only we could see.

Date: 1976

Is It My Imagination?

Have I found a kindred spirit,
Have I found a mating soul,
Is it my imagination
Or has your love just made me whole?

Did your smile just light my night up.
Did your song just warm my day,
Is it my imagination
Or does your love just work that way?

Did your hands just ease my body,
Did your eyes just touch my soul,
Is it my imagination
Or did your love just make me whole?

Did your words just lift my worries,
Did your kiss just ease my mind,
Is it my imagination
Or is your love the curing kind?

Did your lovin' take me higher
Than an eagle ever flew,
Is it my imagination
Am I really one with you?

Yes, I've found a kindred spirit;
Yes, I've found my mating soul.
It's not my imagination
That your love has made me whole.

Date: 22 December 1984

Upsetting My Tranquility

Chorus: So look here, ma'm,
Don't hassle me,
Upsetting my
Tranquility.
I'm just the way
I want to be;
Life's just the way
It aught to be.

I know my homework
Ain't all done;
I stayed out "til
The morning sun.
And what's life for
But havin' fun?

Chorus: So look here, teach,
Don't hassle…

I know my room's
Disaster plus,
But, mom, don't make
A nasty fuss…
It's too late now
I'll miss my bus.

Chorus: So look here, mom,
Don't hassle…

I know the music's
Way too loud;
It keeps me here
Upon my cloud,
Away from all
That god dam crowd.

Chorus: So look here, dad,
Don't hassle.....

I'm sitting here
Just smoking pot,
And doin' things
That I should not...
Just wishing that.
The world would stop.

Chorus. So look here, man,
Don't hassle....

I'm sure you'd make
A lovely wife,
But you don't fit
Into my life,
So give some other
Guy the strife.

Chorus: So look here, girl,
Don't hassle....

Date: 5 April 1977
Footnote: I wrote this for Bryan and his friend Paul Peterson..to put music to for their band.

Rap for a Valentine

Moma's wearin' rubber boots
and pop can't even swim.
Bro's hittin' on my little sis
so I gotta beat on him.

Teach says I got a attitude
that don't sit well on him.
But I knows that in his bottom drawer
he hides a jar of gin.

There's weepin' in the cellars
and screamin' in the street,
But no one smells the smoke and blood
behind their i-pod beat.

Who's caring for the wretched
while the seas are set to boil?
As long as boss man gets his limo
and has his gas and oil.

The world is all goin' crazy now
we're goin' down the drain.
So bad I can not think no more
it's messin' up my brain.

I can not even try to cope
it's never goin' to end.
I see everybody messin' up
and you're my only friend.

So hop into my rubber boat
we'll grab a hook and line.
We'll fish and dream a day away;
you'll be my valentine.

For Cole with love and hope that you enjoy it.. Grampa

Date: 4 Feb 2008
Footnote: This is a Rap Riff written for Cole. It started in McDonalds in Stittsville one night in February 2008 when we were fooling around listening to some rap accompanied by violins I rhymed off the first two lines which put Cole in stitches laughing...so here I am trying to finish it

(1) Note: The third and fourth stanzas were added on 5 April 2008 prior to meeting with Cole to go to the Kanata Theatre.
They add a more serious tone to the riff.

Night Errands

Nothing warms the soul
Or fills the hole
Like a coffee
Brewed just right.
But you pay the price
In this land of ice
When you drink
That brew at night.

As you grow old
in this land of cold
Mother nature
Takes her toll.
And you know, sometime,
Out of sleep sublime
Out of bed
You'll have roll.

For the faded light
And the icy night
Makes the bladder
Draw up tight;
And it's nature's way
To make you pay
For livin' life
Not right.

You hit hard bare floor
When it's no more
Than minus
Forty-four.
And you leave warm sheets
For a frozen seat
Behind a drafty
Outhouse door.

But take this cup
And fill 'er up
With brew
At any time.
It's a special jug
For your ugly mug
So you no longer
Need to whine.

Don't leave warm sheets
For ice cold seats
"cause this jug
Will improve your lot.
With its flared out rim
It will also serve
As an elegant
Chamber pot

Date: 10 July 1994
Footnote: Composed for Ron Barkley for his 60 birthday on 11 July. I gave him a huge coffee cup as described.

Times Ephemeral

Memories, far fading memories
Of times that are no more.

Times
We ran along the shore
Or, lying naked in the sun,
Watched the sparkling river in
Between the hills
And through the fields.

Nights
We talked until the dawn:
Or, sitting on a wooded hill.
Listened to the whippoorwill
Across the lake
Beyond the point.

Days
Youth followed every whim;
And life was water, sky, and wind,
And space that had no end.
Days of endless strength
And breath and will to live.

Friends with whom these days were shared
Are gone.
I wonder if they look back and care
As much as I
Who wished those days need never die.

Date: June 1963

Yesterday~Today~Tomorrow

"Today is ours; no more or less have we.
Let us make the most of it."

Yesterday we ran and sang
And laughed until the valley rang:
And oft times might have shed a tear,
But yesterday is no more here.
Yesterday is gone.

Tomorrow we may love and play,
And one has hope for a future day;
Yet no one knows what it may bring;
We only hope 'tis cause to sing.
Tomorrow may not come.

Lose all thought of yesterday;
Fears for the morrow cast away.
Today, and it alone, have we;
A speck in time though it may be,
Today alone is certainty.

Date: July 1956
Footnote: I was working out of the Levis Dockyard doing acceptance tests on the new St. Laurent class Destroyer.

Rose Buds

I wept to think
That I might leave you;

And three drops fell
And froze on rose buds,

So that my love
Could ever stay with you.

Date: 17 Sept 2008
Footnote: I wrote this poem for Josi about 02h00 AM on Wed 17 Sept 2008 in my room at the Queensway Carleton Hospital. She was sleeping in a lounge chair beside my bed. I was near death in an isolation unit for 12 days following a severe reaction to chemotherapy. Josi stayed with me every day and night...a godsend.

Later, on our anniversary day, 9 Oct 2008, I gave the poem to Josi along with two earrings and a necklace, each bearing a rosebud preserved in glass.

My Kiss Is In The Wind

The earth and I are one. I am its wind and water,
its sea and sun. I am its space and time
solidified an instant in eternity, then gone
to elements again.

And you, fair daughter of this same warm earth,
if you would know my kiss, turn your parted lips
to the wind, that I may kiss them soft and gently
in the quiet still of night.

If you would hear my love song, listen to
the songs of flowing streams and bird songs
in the dawn.

If you would feel my touch, press dew dipped roses
to your cheek and wrap your body in the sun warmth
of a summer day.

If you would know my joy in you, see the dance
of star lamps on gently rippled waters and the glory burst
of northern lights on still cool nights of wonder.

I am never gone, my love. I am in all these things
and more. And always, my kiss is in the wind.

Date: 19 May 1972
In July 2010 I dedicated this poem to Tom and Catherine Hanson...
and I am indebted to Catherine for picking the Chagall print that
accompanies it.

Chagall, M. (1969–1970) Saint - Paul Dans La Nuit Bleue